T0413189

All Families

Blended Families

by Tamika M. Murray

FOCUS READERS

BEACON

www.focusreaders.com

Focus Readers is distributed by North Star Editions:
sales@northstareditions.com | 888-417-0195

Produced for Focus Readers by Red Line Editorial.

Photographs ©: Shutterstock Images, cover, 1, 4, 6, 8, 10, 12, 14, 20–21, 29; iStockphoto, 17, 18, 22, 25, 26

Library of Congress Cataloging-in-Publication Data
Names: Murray, Tamika M., author.
Title: Blended families / Tamika M. Murray.
Description: Lake Elmo, MN : Focus Readers, [2023] | Series: All families |
   Includes index. | Audience: Grades 2-3
Identifiers: LCCN 2022032098 (print) | LCCN 2022032099 (ebook) | ISBN
   9781637394571 (hardcover) | ISBN 9781637394946 (paperback) | ISBN
   9781637395660 (pdf) | ISBN 9781637395318 (ebook)
Subjects: LCSH: Stepfamilies--Juvenile literature. | Identity
   (Psychology)--Juvenile literature.
Classification: LCC HQ759.92 .M87 2023 (print) | LCC HQ759.92 (ebook) |
   DDC 306.874/7--dc23/eng/20220815
LC record available at https://lccn.loc.gov/2022032098
LC ebook record available at https://lccn.loc.gov/2022032099

Printed in the United States of America
Mankato, MN
012023

About the Author

Tamika M. Murray is an award-winning author of nonfiction books, a freelance writer, and a certified social worker. She currently resides in Southern New Jersey with her boyfriend and three rambunctious kitties.

Table of Contents

Chapter 1

Blending a Family

A girl sits at the dinner table. Before Dad moved out, Tuesday used to be pasta night. But now, the girl's stepdad makes tacos on Tuesdays. Mom loves the tacos. So does the stepdad's son.

A new meal is a smaller change than a new stepparent. But it may be a sign of the larger change. That can feel hard.

Having meals together is one way for family members to connect with one another.

But the girl doesn't like them. She misses Dad and his pasta dinners.

Mom and the stepdad want the girl to be included in the meals. So, they offer to cook pasta on

Tuesdays. Taco night will be Wednesday instead. And the girl can choose what goes into her tacos.

Blending a family usually leads to changes. Changes can be good. However, they often take time to accept.

Did You Know?

Blended families can plan meals together. That way, each person can help decide what to eat.

Chapter 2

Many Kinds of Families

A blended family forms when a parent marries a new partner. The new partner becomes a stepparent. Sometimes, this new partner does not have their own children.

 More than 1.6 million US couples got married in 2020.

More than one in six US children live with at least one half sibling.

Sometimes, the stepparent does have children. The children of stepparents are called stepsiblings.

Some blended families grow. A baby born into a blended family is a half sibling. Half siblings share one parent.

Blended families form for many reasons. One reason is because of **divorce**. Another reason is if a parent dies. When that happens, death creates a loss in the family. But blended families can cope with changes. They can deal with the pain together.

Did You Know?

In the United States, approximately 1,300 new blended families are formed each day.

Chapter 3

Changes and Choices

All families go through good and bad times. Blended families have challenges, too. If a parent dies, kids need to **grieve**. They need time to heal. It may take even longer to get used to a stepparent.

 People grieve in different ways. Some people feel sad or angry. Others don't feel much for a long time.

13

 Sharing can be hard for all siblings.

A child with no stepsiblings may struggle. The child might feel nervous when a stepparent is around. The child might want both of their parents close.

Blended families with stepsiblings must deal with changes, too. For instance, some stepsiblings may have to share a bedroom. Sharing a room can be tough. Each child might be used to having their own bedroom. They might struggle with losing their privacy. Learning to live with other kids can cause fights.

Some tough moments can take place in the morning. **Routines** may change. For example, maybe Mom used to make everyone breakfast. Maybe Dad used to ask trivia questions on the way to school. But Mom and Dad aren't together anymore. Now the stepdad makes breakfast. And the car ride to school is filled with music, not trivia. Routines offer a sense of security. For this reason, changes to those routines can cause **stress**.

Yet new routines can help blended families grow closer. Mom and the stepdad could read the bedtime story together. They might

 Stress that lasts a long time can lead to headaches.

start doing that every other night.

Plus, kids can help make decisions

about a new routine. For instance,

they could help choose bedtimes.

These choices help kids have some control.

Having choices can also help kids who live in multiple homes. One parent might live alone. The other might live with a stepparent's family. The kid might live at each home for part of the time.

Kids switch homes on **transition days**. These days can cause stress. As a result, kids might want to do an activity or have a meal before leaving. Getting to choose can make the day less stressful. It also shows kids their opinions matter.

Did You Know?

In the United States, Stepmother's Day is celebrated on the third Sunday in May.

Different Looks

Having a **mixed-race** blended family can bring up extra challenges. Strangers might stare at kids in blended families. They may ask questions if stepsiblings have different skin colors. Questions about skin color can hurt. Also, kids may get confused when people stare.

Confused kids often need to talk about their feelings. They can also embrace what makes them different. For some kids, it's their skin color and hair. Family meetings can help work through some of these challenges. Talking allows people to share their feelings.

In 2020, approximately 1 in 10 people in the United States were mixed-race.

Chapter 4

All Families Are Different

Coming together as a blended family takes practice. It takes time, too. It's okay if things are done differently. For instance, eating together offers time for talking. Talking can help fix problems.

Blended families can build deep connections with one another.

Some children may think they cannot share their feelings. But that can make problems worse.

There are other ways to **communicate**, too. Kids can do arts and crafts with a stepparent. They might color or paint. These activities let them show emotions **creatively**. Playing sports or games can also be helpful. People can talk with one another while having fun. Older kids can help the younger kids play.

 Creative activities can help people in blended families learn more about each other.

Some ideas can help children get used to new spaces. Kids might pick out a place in the new home. It could be a chair in the living room.

 It can be very important for people to have a place that is all their own.

That spot will be just for them. Kids might even be able to decorate the area. Then they can use it for studying or relaxing. This kind of area can help if kids are sharing a bedroom. It can also help make transition days easier.

Blended families may be different from other families. But being different isn't bad. It doesn't matter how they look. It doesn't matter what brought them together. Blended families are still families.

Did You Know?

September 16 is National Stepfamily Day in the United States.

FOCUS ON
Blended Families

Write your answers on a separate piece of paper.

1. Write a paragraph describing the main ideas of Chapter 2.

2. What are some routines in your day? Do they feel important to you? Why or why not?

3. What can help children get used to a blended family?

    A. having no routines

    B. making their own choices

    C. not communicating

4. What is one way that blended families can form?

    A. The same parents have another child.

    B. One parent dies, and the other does not remarry.

    C. Parents get divorced, and one remarries.

5. What does **cope** mean in this book?

*But blended families can **cope** with changes. They can deal with the pain together.*

    A. to work through and accept
    B. to keep things the same
    C. to be happy alone

6. What does **security** mean in this book?

*Routines offer a sense of **security**. For this reason, changes to those routines can cause stress.*

    A. an activity someone does regularly
    B. a calm feeling that things will be okay
    C. a guard or police officer

Answer key on page 32.

Glossary

communicate
To make something known to others.

creatively
Using the imagination, often to make art.

divorce
A process where two people decide to stop being married.

grieve
To feel deep sadness or pain over a loss.

mixed-race
When a person is made up of two or more ethnic backgrounds.

routines
Sets of actions people do regularly.

stress
The body and mind's responses to difficult situations.

transition days
Days when a child leaves one parent's home to stay at another parent's home.

To Learn More

BOOKS

Houser, Grace. *What's Life Like in a Blended Family?* New York: PowerKids Press, 2019.

Lynch, Amy. *Understanding Families: Feelings, Fighting & Figuring It Out.* Middleton, WI: American Girl Publishing, 2019.

Olsher, Sara. *Nothing Stays the Same, but That's Okay: A Book to Read When Everything (or Anything) Changes.* Santa Rosa, CA: Mighty + Bright, 2021.

NOTE TO EDUCATORS

Visit **www.focusreaders.com** to find lesson plans, activities, links, and other resources related to this title.

Index

A
activities, 19, 24

C
changes, 7, 11, 15–16
children, 9–10, 19, 24–25

D
divorce, 11

F
feelings, 13–14, 20, 24

L
loss, 11, 13

M
marriage, 9
meals, 6–7, 19, 23
mixed-race families, 20

P
parents, 9–11, 13–16, 18

R
rooms, 15, 25, 27
routines, 15–17

S
sharing, 10, 15, 20, 24, 27
stepparent, 5–6, 9–10,
    13–14, 16, 18–19, 24
stepsiblings, 10,
    14–15, 20
stress, 16, 19

T
transition days, 19, 27

Answer Key: 1. Answers will vary; **2.** Answers will vary; **3.** B; **4.** C; **5.** A; **6.** B